A Birthday Present for

DANIEL

A Birthday Present for

DANIEL

A CHILD'S STORY OF LOSS

by Juliet Rothman

Illustrated by
Louise Gish

Prometheus Books

59 John Glenn Drive
Amherst, NewYork 14228-2197

Note to Parents: In order to preserve and protect
our environment and its creatures,
please use biodegradable balloons!

Published 1996 by Prometheus Books

00 99 98 97 96   5 4 3 2 1

Library of Congress Cataloging-in-Publication Data

Rothman, Juliet Cassuto, 1942–
    A birthday present for Daniel : a child's story of loss / Juliet C.
Rothman ; illustrations by Louise Gish.
        p.   cm.
    Summary: A young girl whose brother has died describes how
she feels and tells about some of the things her family does to help
them accept his death.
    ISBN 1–57392–054–1 (cloth)
    [1. Death—Fiction. 2. Brothers and sisters—Fiction. 3. Grief—
Fiction.] I. Gish, Louise, ill. II. Title.
PZ7.R744Bi   1996
[E]—dc20   96–4277
                                                              CIP
                                                              AC

Printed in the United States of America on acid-free paper

For my daughters
Susan and Debbie
and for
everyone who has
lost a brother or sister

When my brother, Daniel, died, I cried and cried.
My mom did, too.

My dad and sister said it hurt too much to cry.

Lots of times, I wear his clothes under mine.
I pick his favorite lunches, pizza and hot dogs,
in the school cafeteria.

I go to his room all by myself
and hug Chocolate Milk, his teddy bear.
Sometimes I climb into his bed and pull his covers
over my head.

After a while, I cry.

I don't want to be with any of my friends
who have brothers,
even my best friend, Christie.

It makes me cry when I am with them.

My sister, Debbie, doesn't do any of these things.
She doesn't wear his clothes or hug his teddy bear
or eat his favorite food in the cafeteria.

My mom says everybody hurts,
but people show their hurt in different ways.
Just because Debbie's way is different doesn't mean
she hurts any less or any more than I do.

My mom says we all hurt.

Nobody in our family knows how to act anymore.

Everything is all mixed up.

Sometimes I get upset at everybody, even at Daniel.
I know it's not his fault that he died,
but I get angry anyway.

I used to sit between my dad and Daniel at dinner.

Now I sit between my dad and Debbie.

We used to take turns getting
our goodnight kisses from Mom and Dad.

It was my turn to be last every third night.
I loved being last.
Now it's my turn every other night,
but it's not the same.

Sometimes, when I wake up in the morning,
I forget that Daniel is not in his room.

I know Debbie forgets, too, because sometimes I see her open the door to his room and look in to see if he is there.

I know she wishes he was.

Now my dad is the only boy in our family.
I don't think he likes it too much.

Even our dog, Josie, is a girl.

Tacky, the hamster, is a boy,
but Dad doesn't play with Tacky much.

My mom is sad all the time.

I don't think she cares as much about me anymore.

I used to get angry at Daniel a lot.

He teased me,

and sometimes, when we fought,

he hit me and it hurt.

Sometimes

I used to wish he would go away

and never come back.

Now he really has gone away,

and I want him to come back.

I want him to come back so I can say I'm sorry.

Even birthdays are different now.

We always get to choose
the kind of cake we want,
and my mom makes them.

Last year, Debbie wanted a flower cake and
Daniel chose a football cake
and I picked a rocket ship cake.

Daniel used to love his birthday best
of all the days of the year.

He loved to get presents.

This year, Mom said we could have
a birthday party for Daniel, anyway.

A very special kind of birthday party,
with very special presents.

After school on Daniel's birthday,
Mom and Dad and Debbie and I
went to a party store to buy some balloons.
We each picked two balloons.

At home, we wrote secret messages
to Daniel on little pieces of paper.
Then we tied the messages to the strings
right under the balloons.

I can't tell you what I wrote in mine because it's a secret.

We went outside.

It was getting dark,
and it was very quiet and still.

We sang "Happy Birthday" to Daniel.

I looked up at the balloons.
I could see all the messages tied underneath.

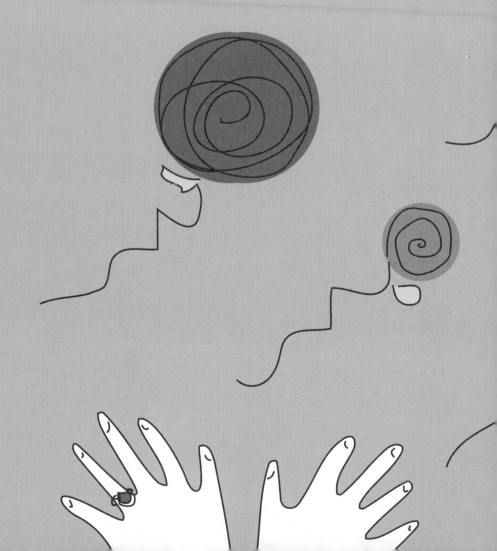

Then we let them go.

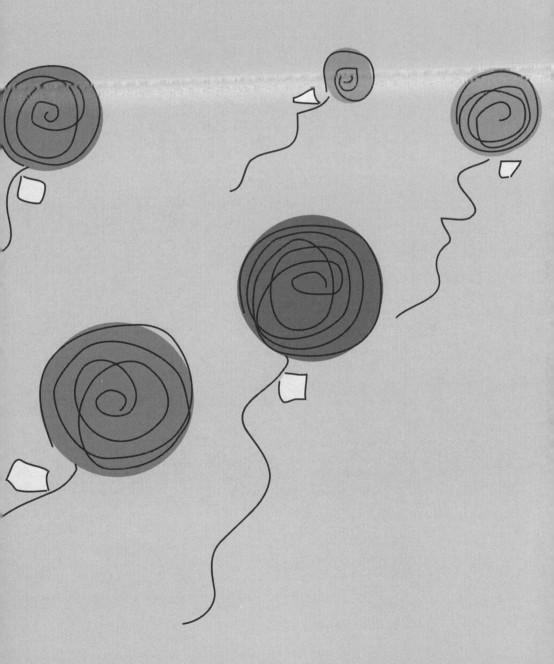

I watched all the balloons go up in the sky.

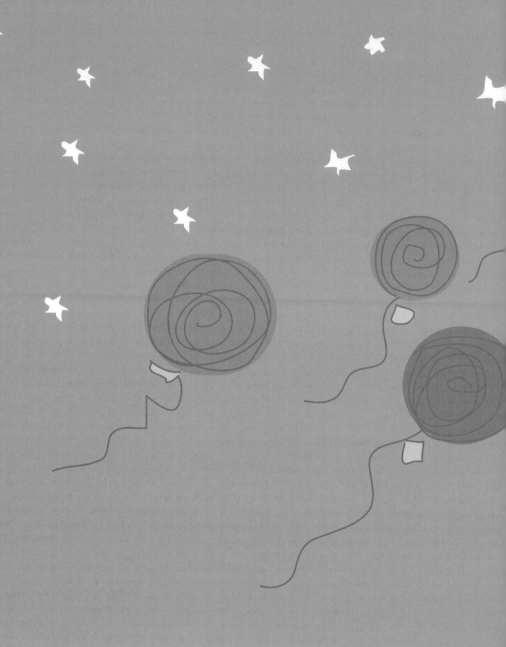

They went up slowly, and it took a long time.

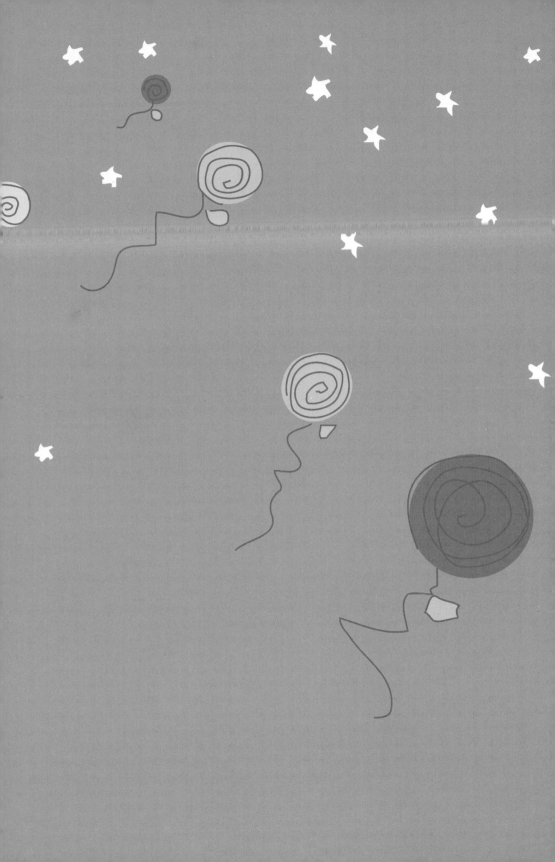

I kept watching until all the balloons were gone
and the sky was all dark
and I could see the stars shining.

It was a very special birthday.